For my sweet Belle, who never ever EVER
wants to go to bed. - C.M.

For my beloved children, who always inspire me, and for my strong and
independent homeland, Ukraine, which is always in my heart. - T.M.

Special thanks to Jimmy and Abby Althoff
for their encouragement, love, and support.

Starry Mill Entertainment, LLC.
www.starrymill.com

ISBN 9781940733043 (paperback)

Starry Mill Entertainment, LLC. • San Francisco

GO TO BED, FRED!

WRITTEN BY CARLY MOTTINGER
ILLUSTRATED BY TANYA MATIIKIV

This is my dog, Fred. He's my very best friend.
There's one thing you should know about him:
he hates going to bed.

This is Fred's bed. See the sign I made?
It spells his name: **F-R-E-D**.

It takes a lot of work to get Fred ready for bed.
First, I have to help him clean up his toys.
Fred is very messy.

Next, I help Fred put on his pajamas.
Doesn't he look cute?

"Who's a good boy?"

Okay, maybe we can skip
the pajamas tonight.

Fred loves a bowl of warm
milk to help him sleep.

But I'm only allowed to give
him water because, as it turns
out, milk makes him poop.
A lot.
I learned that lesson
the hard way.

Anyhoo . . .

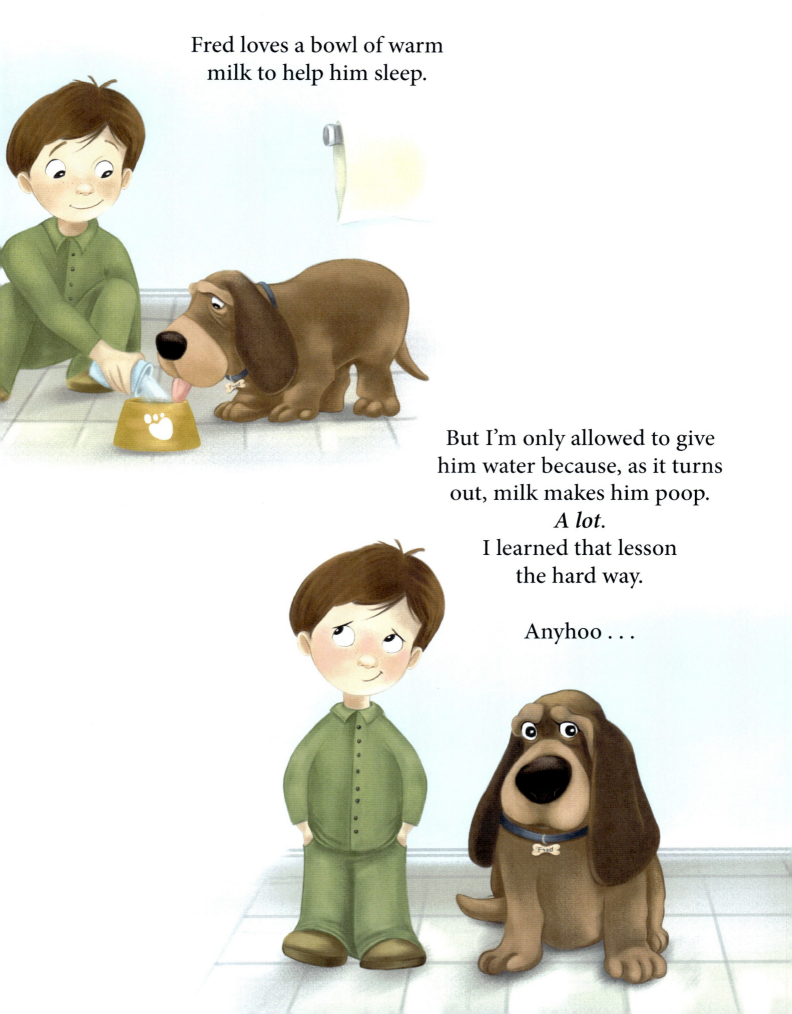

Once he's had a drink of water, it's time to give Fred his special once-a-day treat from the vet. It's how Fred brushes his teeth.

It doesn't really help with his dog breath, though.

Next, we move on to bedtime stories.
I'm teaching Fred to read. I think it's going well.

When reading time is over, I put on a little
bedtime show for Fred. He's a great audience.
"What do you call a dog who gets left out in
the sun? A hot dog!!!
Get it, Fred?"

"Wait a minute,
is this thing even on?"

It's a lot of work being a dog dad.
"Hey Fred, wait for me!"

Do you want to know a little secret about Fred?
He still needs his fuzzy blanket to fall asleep even though
he's about eighty-six in human years. Or something like that.
I haven't completely figured out dog math yet.

My favorite part of Fred's bedtime routine is singing his goodnight songs. I mostly make them up, but it seems like he enjoys it when I sing really high and play really loud. See how sleepy he gets?

Finally, Fred gets two hugs
and two kisses.

He also likes it when I lie next to him
for eleventy-nine minutes.
Man, bedtime is exhausting. Am I right?

Before I go to my room, I wish Fred sweet dreams.
I nicely say that the kitchen is closed,
so he's not allowed to have any more snacks.

I tell him that he can ask me all his questions tomorrow.
He has a lot: "Do sharks take baths?
What are bones made out of?
Why are there so many snails?"

I show him that there are no monsters in the closet.
I remind him that three nightlights are plenty bright.
And no, he can't sleep in my bed with me because he's a
big dog, and big dogs need to sleep in their own beds.

I explain that even though falling asleep can be hard,
he can do hard things.

Hey, I think I hear
my mom calling me!

"Brody! Time for bed!!!"

That's me. My name is Brody.
Lucky for my mom,
I'm super easy to put to bed.

"Coming, Mom!"

"Come on, Brody Bug. It's time for bed."

"Sure, Mom, I just put Fred to bed. Boy, is it A LOT of work. Good thing it's really easy to put me to bed! Right, Mom?!"

Wait!! Before I go, I should probably clean up the playroom real quick.

The kitchen table sure could use a scrub. "Hey! Fred! Why aren't you in bed?

Since we're both awake, how about we do a big, messy art project?!"

"No more activites, Brody. It's time to go upstairs."

"Sure, no problem, Mom. Looks like Fred will be joining us. Between you and me, he's impossible to put to bed. Anyhoo, I'm ready to go change my pajamas five times."

"I've got a feeling you're going to LOVE the books I picked out for story time tonight.

Should we go get my glass of water? I want to make sure it's not too cold. Or too watery.

Speaking of water . . . how deep is a puddle? Do penguins have ears? Are farts just burps from your butt? Why are elbows so wrinkly?"

"Blrblgh flooob grrr shmoosh? Plurkkee globshmood?"

"Why is the moon called the moon? Do fish have eyebrows? Why do people have to sleep, anyway?"

After fourteen stories . . .

six games . . .

four songs . . .

one blanket fort . . .

a round of blocks . . .

and three puppet shows,
I decided I was finally
ready to . . .

. . . break my headstand record!

"That's enough for tonight, Brody.
It really is time to go to bed."

Mom wishes me sweet dreams and tells me that the kitchen is closed.
She says I can ask her all my questions tomorrow.

She shows me there are no monsters in the closet and promises
that my three nightlights are plenty bright.

She gives me a kiss and reminds me that I'm a big boy,
and big boys need to sleep in their own beds.

Mom knows falling asleep can be hard,
but she tells me I can do hard things.

"Mom, before you go . . . was that a yes or a no on the big messy art project? Also, remember that rock I lost? Now would be the perfect time for us to go look for it."

"Good night, Brody. I love you. See you in the morning."

I should probably go check on Fred.
He never wants to go to bed.

Maybe after I rest my eyes
for a minute or two . . .

Carly Mottinger grew up in Northern California before moving to Los Angeles, where she earned an MFA from the USC School of Cinematic Arts. After receiving her graduate degree, Carly worked as a staff writer for Nickelodeon and sold her first children's book (*Lights, Camera, Lexi!*) to Disney Junior. Carly is a member of the Writers Guild of America West. She currently resides in Northern California with her husband and four daughters.

Tanya Matiikiv is a children's book illustrator from Ukraine. She is a mother of two wonderful children who inspire her illustrations. Since childhood, she has been fascinated by art and painting. After graduating from Zaporizhzhya Music College and Zaporizhzhya National University, she continued her studies in the studio of the outstanding Ukrainian artist Anton Sheretov. She has worked as a children's book illustrator since 2015 and feels fortunate to have such an inspiring job.

Made in the USA
Monee, IL
17 May 2023

33442309R00024